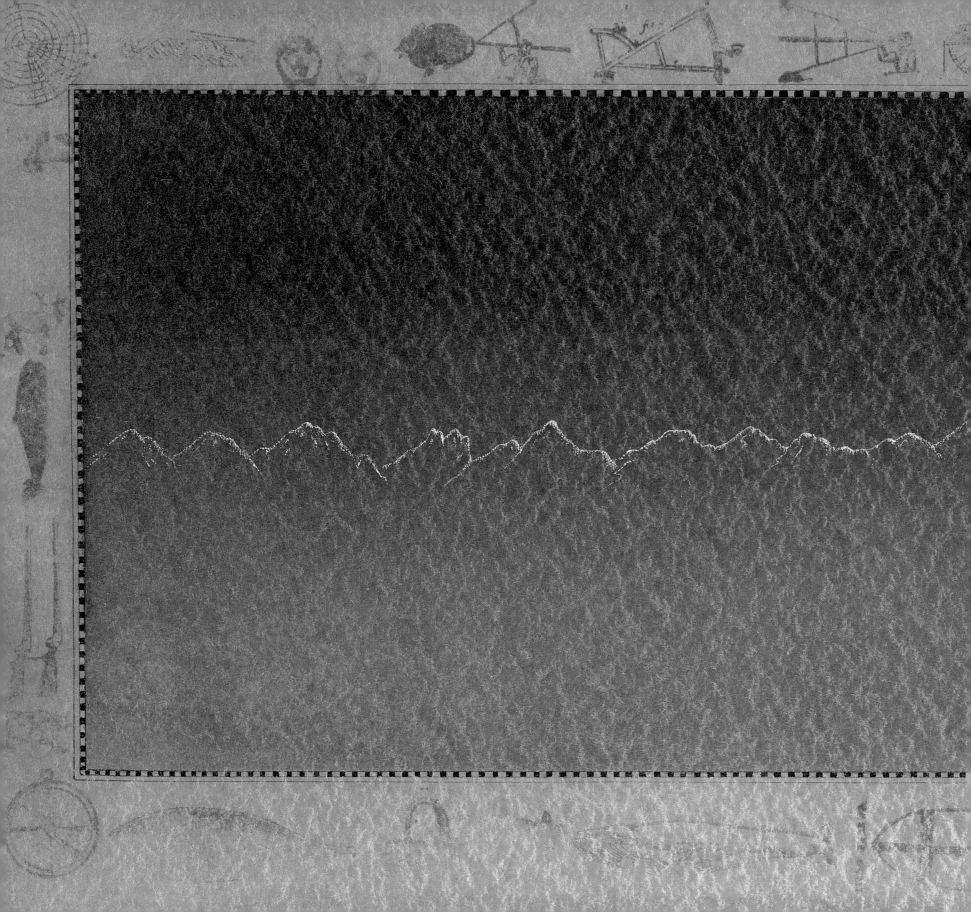

A Small Tall Tale from the Far Far North

by Peter Sís

A GROUNDWOOD BOOK

DOUGLAS & McINTYRE TORONTO VANCOUVER

My hero was alone; I could not have done this book alone. I want to thank:

My brother, David, who brought up the idea and reminded me of our childhood enchantment.

My father, Vladimir, Moravian explorer himself, who pointed me in the right direction.

My editor, Frances Foster, who once again navigated the stormy seas of my creativity.

My wife, Terry Lajtha, who most of all saved the project while bringing forth a greater one.

My daughter, Madeleine, who came into the world just in time to encourage me to finish the book.

In doing the illustrations for this book, I consulted everything I could find on the people of
the Arctic, their customs, and their culture. Especially helpful were Charlotte and David Yue's fine book,
The Igloo (Houghton Mifflin, 1988); the New York Public Library Picture Collection;
the National Geographic Society; the University of Alaska at Anchorage;
the Baidarka Society; and the rich portfolio of Eskimo drawings
collected in the early 1900s by Robert Flaherty.

Copyright © 1993 by Peter Sís
First Groundwood Books edition, 2001
Published simultaneously in the USA by Farrar, Straus and Giroux, 2001
Originally published in 1993 by Alfred A. Knopf, Inc.,
New York, and simultaneously in Canada by Random House of
Canada Limited, Toronto

Groundwood Books / Douglas & McIntyre
720 Bathurst Street, Suite 500
Toronto, Ontario M5S 2R4

We acknowledge the financial support of the Canada Council for the
Arts, the Ontario Arts Council and the Government of Canada
through the Book Publishing Industry Development Program for our
publishing activities.

Canadian Cataloguing in Publication Data

Sís, Peter
A small tall tale from the far Far North
"A Groundwood book".
ISBN 0-88899-431-1
I. Title.
PZ7.S574Sm 2001   j813'.54   C00-932395-3

Visit us on the World Wide Web at
www.groundwoodbooks.com

Designed by Ed Miller
Printed and bound in the United States of America
by Berryville Graphics

Jan Welzl was a folk hero in my native Czechoslovakia when I was growing up. Tales of his breathtaking Arctic journeys inspired me—and countless others—to dream of similar adventures.

In 1893 life in Central Europe was difficult; the political landscape was changing, and many people were unemployed. According to his own account, Jan Welzl, a twenty-five-year-old locksmith, was eager to escape a world that seemed gray and hopeless. "With a good pair of hands I can survive and maybe find my fortune somewhere else," he wrote. He would travel overland, across Siberia, to the Far North.

By working on a construction crew for the Trans-Siberian Railway, he earned enough money to buy a small horse and a cart with a false bottom (for hiding his belongings from robbers, he said). He also bought tools, hunting gear, and food.

He traveled without a map, adjusting his route according to the information he picked up along the way. When he reached a river and there was no bridge or ferry, he built a raft to carry him and his horse and cart across. When he encountered escaped political prisoners who were hiding in the wilderness, he used his locksmith tools to free them from their leg shackles. When he got closer to the polar region, he traded his horse and cart for reindeer and sled. He met every obstacle and problem with a solution, and after three long winters he reached the Bering Sea and St. Lawrence Island.

Jan Welzl referred to all the native peoples of the Arctic by their common European name: Eskimo. But the people he met on St. Lawrence Island were probably Yupik; and in the Yukon Territory they were most likely Inuit.

Here is a fragment of Jan Welzl's story (a tall tale?), as it has grown in my imagination . . .

Peter Sís
New York City

Oh, misery! There must be a better life than this.
I'm going to find it.

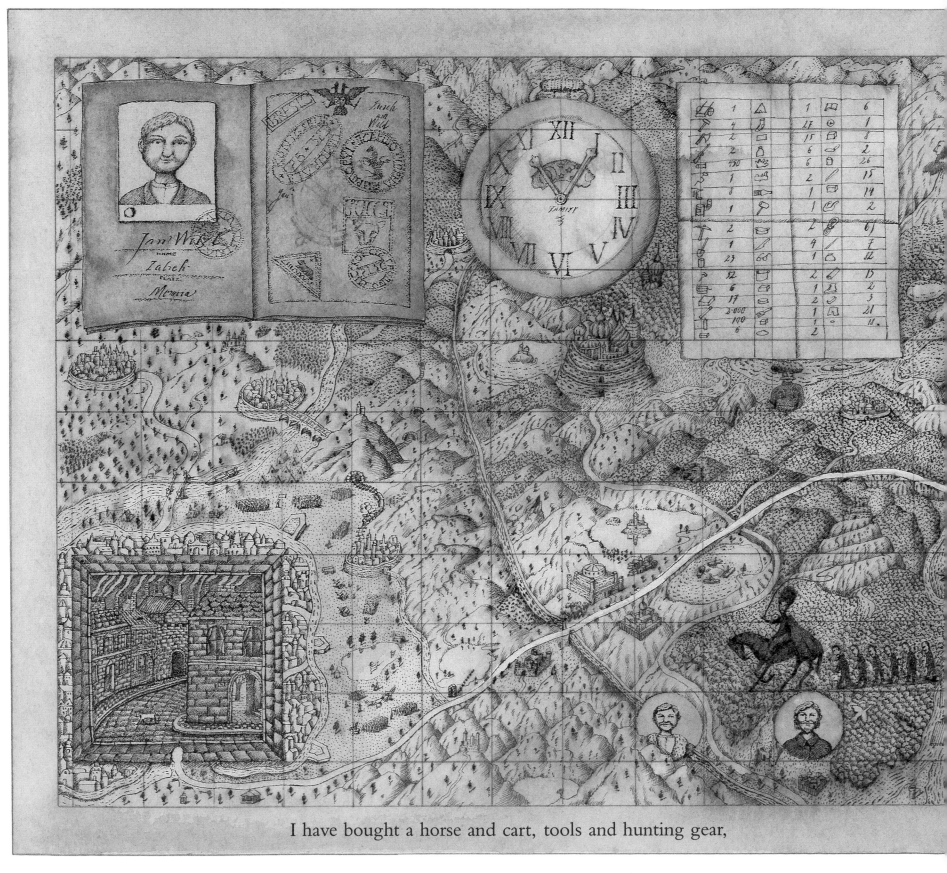

I have bought a horse and cart, tools and hunting gear,

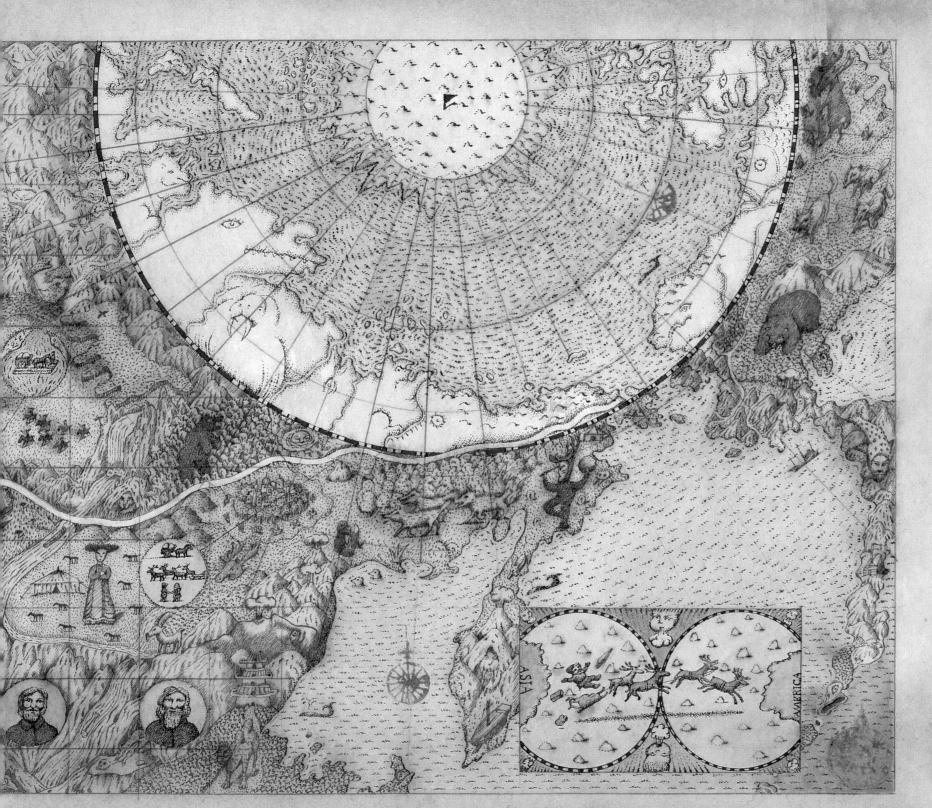

food and provisions, and I am heading for the Far North.

I had to trade my dear horse for reindeer and sled. It was a tearful good-bye after three years together. Now I am galloping southward over the frozen Bering Sea. The reindeer fly across the ice while my sled bounces over the irregular surface. From time to time we stop to look around for any signs of life. As far as I can see, there is nothing but snow and ice and wide open space. At last I feel free.

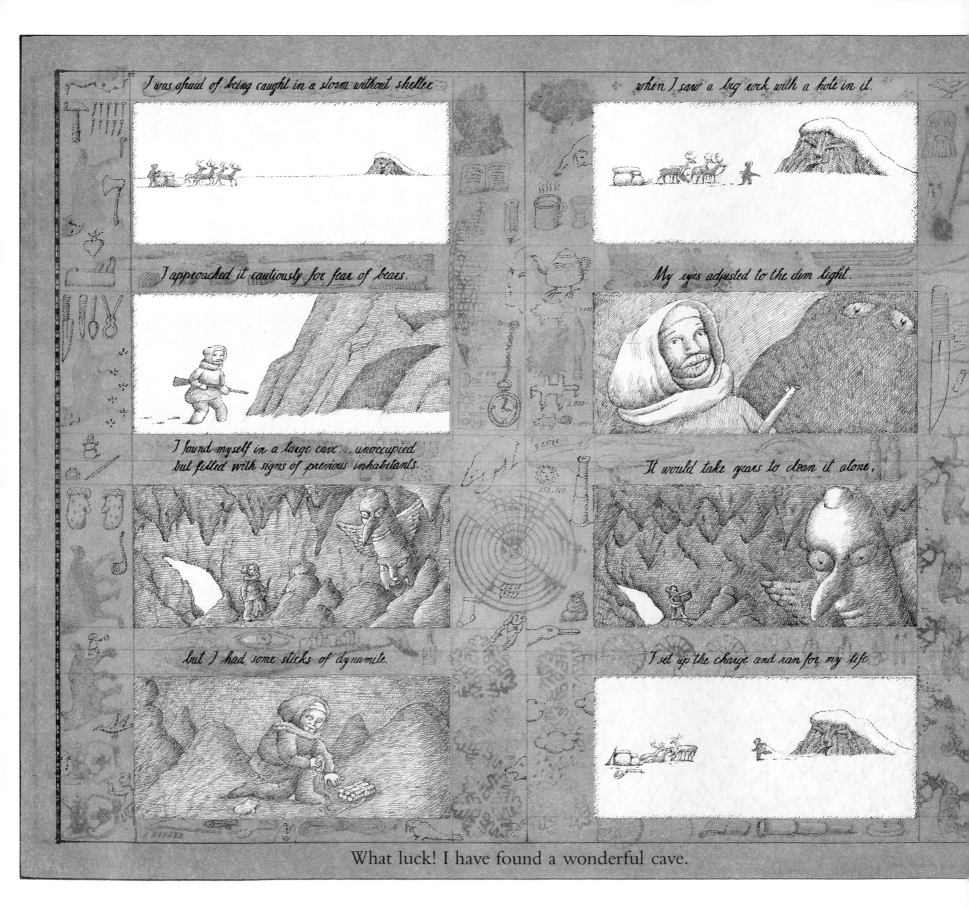

What luck! I have found a wonderful cave.

just in time.

The entrance was bigger

and the inside much enlarged.

From the rubble I found wood to make a good strong door.

I tidied up the cave, closed off the space for the reindeer, built a bed and a fireplace,

and soon had a comfortable home.

Getting fresh food proved more of a problem

and required both patience and skill.

With a bit of work it will make a good home.

I had expected to find Eskimos here, but I have not
seen another living soul. I am very much alone.

One day while checking my traps, I see a strange glow on the horizon.

I think I have found gold, so I go eagerly toward it.

Then, all of a sudden, I am flying.

I end up stuck fast to the mountain with my sled, my traps, and all my belongings. Only now do I remember the stories about a magnetic stone said to be some sort of meteorite. You have to heat it with a bonfire to break its magnetic power. But I am alone, hanging head down, under my traps and gun, getting colder and colder…

A great drowsiness comes over me.

I hear voices, as in a dream. Then my body is pried loose from the mountain and lifted onto a kayak.

At first I think my rescuers are angels from heaven. But they are hunters, who have saved me from almost certain death.

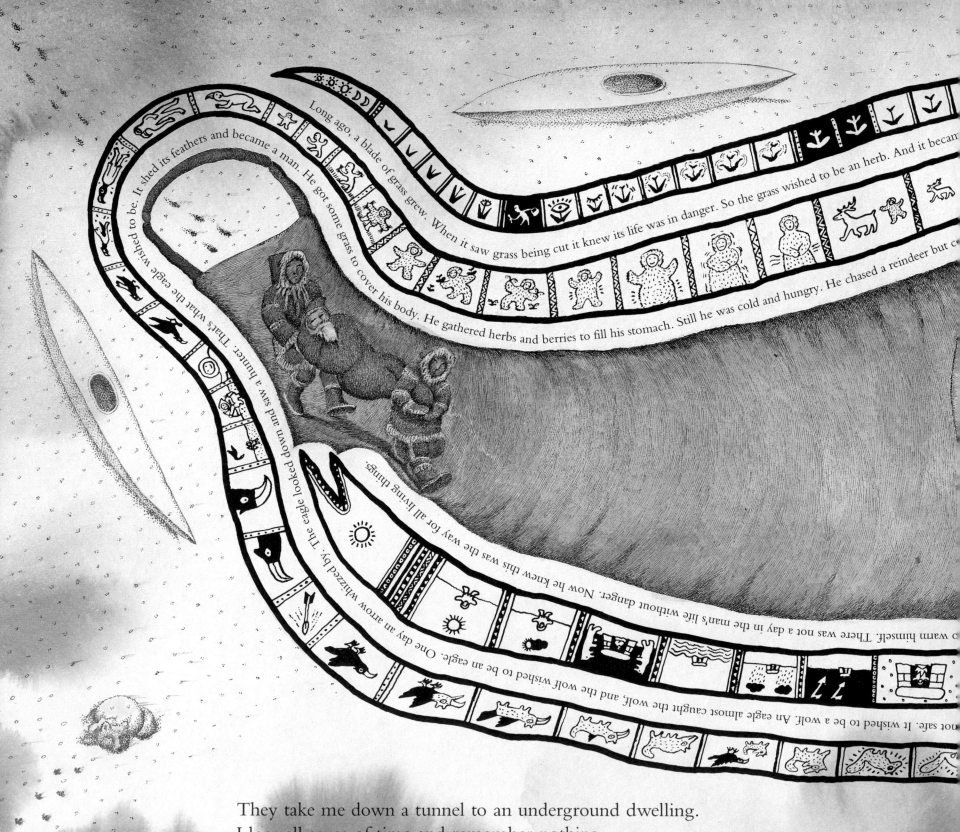

Long ago, a blade of grass grew. When it saw grass being cut it knew its life was in danger. So the grass wished to be an herb. And it became an herb. He gathered herbs and berries to fill his stomach. Still he was cold and hungry. He chased a reindeer but could not warm himself. There was not a day in the man's life without danger. Now he knew this was the way for all living things. One day an arrow whizzed by. The eagle looked down and saw a hunter. That's what the eagle wished to be. It shed its feathers and became a man. He got some grass to cover his body. It wished to be a wolf. An eagle almost caught the wolf, and the wolf wished to be an eagle. It wished to be a wolf.

They take me down a tunnel to an underground dwelling.
I lose all sense of time and remember nothing.

Later I learn the songs and tales that were whispered
to me while I was coming back to life.

They surround me with their trusting friendliness.

I have never met such kind people.

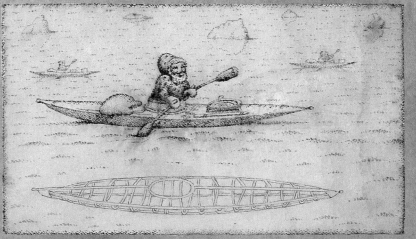

How to make a watertight kayak and capsize and right myself without getting wet.

How to sneak up on a bear and use a spear thrower.

How to trap seals at the breathing hole and fish at the mouth of a river.

They are teaching me everything they know.

How to dress warmly and join in the fun. How to engrave whalebone and use an _ulu_ (the women's all purpose knife).

How to make frames for tents and cooking and drying racks and keep a fire going.

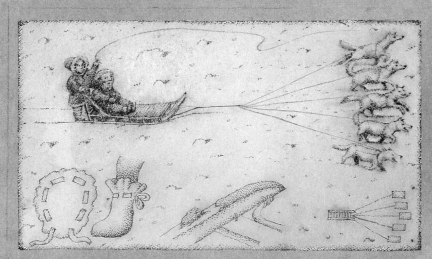

How to hitch a dog team in fan formation, keep their feet warm, and make sled runners slick.

I am learning how to live in this harsh climate.

I try to help my new friends in every way I can. I explain that spring is not magically brought by the polar bird.

I have many ideas for easing their hard lives. I am writing
to the famous American inventor Edison to order
phonographs with recordings of animal sounds.

Still, they enjoy themselves and live in harmony with nature.

But I fear for them—they are very trusting of strangers.

Gold diggers are arriving in great numbers.

Oh! I can see that they will bring trouble with their guns and their whiskey.

How can I get them to leave my friends in peace?

The glowing golden mountain! I will show them the way…

Jan Welzl stayed in the Arctic for thirty years, traveling throughout Alaska, northern Canada, and Siberia. "After years and years of dreadful suffering and privation," he wrote, "from a simple locksmith, sailor, and tramp I became a hunter of note and an established trader, proprietor of a splendid boat, and the chief judge of New Siberia." He learned much from the native people. In return, he tried to defend them against exploitation by foreigners who came with the gold rush and the fur trade.

At some point, Welzl and friends started their own trading company. They bought a ship and in 1924 sailed for San Francisco with a full cargo of furs. Unfortunately, the ship sank off the coast of California. Welzl and his crew were rescued, but Welzl's unusual appearance combined with his almost unintelligible language—a strange mixture of broken English, Russian, German, Czech, and Arctic dialects—and his lack of identification papers made immigration officials suspicious of him. He was deported to Moravia, the country of his birth, which had since become part of Czechoslovakia.

But Jan Welzl had never intended to return to Europe. The Arctic had become his home, and he spent years raising money to get back there—and this is how we know about him today. For it was during this period in Europe that he found an eager audience for the fantastic stories he told about his experiences. He wrote several books, including *Thirty Years in the Golden North*, which I read and enjoyed when I was a boy.

When I was trying to verify where Welzl might have traveled and which Arctic peoples he might have met, I consulted many scholars. In the opinion of some, Jan Welzl was simply a Baron von Münchausen—a teller of tall travel tales—and one even questioned whether such a person had existed at all. Others didn't doubt the truth of his existence or his travels but acknowledged the exaggeration in his stories.

This set me to thinking about my memories of Welzl's memoirs. As a young boy, I could not fully comprehend the Arctic world his books described, but I could well imagine it and never doubted that all his adventures were true. Though I now realize how fantastic and improbable some of them are, for me Jan Welzl, the young man who went to the Far North looking for adventure, will always be real. And as I reread his books, I discover their essence: a curiosity about life, courage, decency, and a love of nature. This is what impressed me as a child and has once again fired my imagination.

There is a gravestone in Dawson, in the Yukon Territory, bearing the name of Jan Welzl and the date of his death, August 15, 1948. He was born on August 15, 1868, in Zábřeh, Moravia.